CONTENTS

CHAPTER 1
ENGLAND DREAMS

The score flashed up on the TV screen.

England 0 – France 1.

"Not again," groaned Leo Diamond as he and his best mate, Mac, slumped back down on the sofa.

"I can't believe we got our hopes up," muttered Mac.

"I can't believe that England goal didn't count," said Leo. "I thought goal-line technology was supposed to be a good thing."

"It must have been weird without it, though," said Mac. "What if the ref and his assistants didn't see exactly where the ball landed?"

"They'd probably just give it to the

other side!" said Leo.

Mac managed a laugh. "Why can't England just learn from other countries?"

"Yeah, look at Germany. They were terrible at Euro 2000 and 2004, and after they changed their football coaching they won the World Cup in 2014," said Leo.

"I wish England would win something in our lifetime," sighed Mac. "We need some decent strikers. We need someone who can smash the ball into the back of the net in the big games."

"Well, if the England team don't have any hotshot players, I guess it's up to us to become them," grinned Leo.

"You're on," said Mac, picking a football up off the carpet. "And if only one of us can make it, it's going to be me."

Mac stood up and started running towards the door.

"In your dreams!" cried Leo, racing after him.

CHAPTER 2
CENTRE-FORWARD GOAL

Whack! Leo let the ball bounce and took it on the half volley. His shot was powerful and accurate, but it was too near the goalkeeper, who in this case was Mac. Mac caught the ball and rolled it back out to Leo.

They were behind the garages near Leo's flat. The ground was oily and bumpy — not a great playing surface — but at least no one else was around.

"I'm going to try to play centre forward for the next school match, against Heston College on Thursday," said Leo, trapping the ball under his right trainer.

"Go for it," nodded Mac. "You've really improved this term. I reckon Mr Cross might give you your first game, especially as Mustafa is injured."

"Cheers," said Leo. Mustafa was their usual centre forward, and was the team's top scorer. Mac had started a couple of league games against other schools, but Leo had only been an unused sub. "I think I'd have done even better if we'd had Mr Lawson coaching us," added Leo.

"You're probably right," replied Mac. "But with Mr Lawson coaching the senior teams, I don't think we'll get much of a look-in."

Leo took his foot off the ball, stepped back five paces and then sent in a blistering shot with the instep of his right shoe. It was a good strike and it curved forwards, but Mac was up to it. He stretched to his left and punched the ball away. Leo sighed with frustration. How could he ever be a decent centre forward if he couldn't even get any goals past Mac?

"Wow!" cried a voice. "It's Leo Diamond the sharpshooter. School teams around the country should be shaking in their boots."

Leo groaned. The voice belonged to Gavin Mathers, the most irritating kid in his year at school. Gavin strolled towards them.

"Go and hassle someone else!" shouted Mac.

"Why should I, when there are a couple of world-class players to watch here? I heard what you were saying about trying to get centre forward for the next game, Leo."

"It's got nothing to do with you," snapped Leo.

"Oh, but it has," replied Gavin, "because that's exactly the position I'm going for."

Leo's heart sank. Gavin usually played out on the right wing. He

thought he was the best player
on earth, but he'd only made one
appearance for the team so far and
that had been ten minutes as a sub.

"Leo's way better than you," said
Mac. "And Mr Cross knows it."

"So why hasn't he picked Leo for a
single game?" demanded Mac.

"He hasn't seen the best of me yet,"
said Leo.

Gavin burst out laughing. "You don't
stand a chance."

And before Leo or Mac could hit
back, Gavin wandered off with a smug
grin on his face.

Leo snarled, kicking one of the
garage doors. It made a deep rumbling
sound.

"Forget him," said Mac. "He's all

mouth."

But Leo couldn't forget about Gavin.
How humiliating would it be if Gavin
got the centre-forward role and Leo
was rejected?

"I've got to make a move," said Mac,
checking his watch. "Are you coming?"

Leo shook his head. "I'm going to
hang back here a bit and practise my
shooting."

"Cool, see you tomorrow then," said
Mac as he hurried off.

Leo whacked the ball against another
garage door, controlled the rebound
with his instep and hit it again. He'd
been doing this for ten minutes when
he overpowered his shot and the
ball spun away. It landed in some
old cardboard boxes filled with junk.

Leo jogged over to collect his ball. It was lying next to a tatty poster with the England team on it. Suddenly the ground started shaking. It was only a little at first, but quickly became violent.

An earthquake? Round here? "No way," thought Leo. As bits of dirt flicked up at his face, Leo closed his eyes, lost his balance and crashed towards the ground.

CHAPTER 3
LESSONS FROM A LEGEND

When Leo opened his eyes, the ground wasn't shaking at all. He found himself lying on a large patch of grass behind a tall, brick building. Three floors of windows looked out onto the grass.

Leo saw a figure stepping out from a door. At first it was just a shadow, but as the figure moved nearer, Leo could see it was a man with a football under his arm. He was dressed in a grey suit and red tie. There was something about the man that looked familiar, but Leo couldn't place him.

"You must be Leo," said the man, stopping when he was a few metres away.

"And you're...you're..." said Leo, scrambling to his feet and trying to work out how he'd got here.

"This happens far too much," said the man with a sigh that changed into a smile. "My name's Geoff Hurst. Does that ring any bells?"

Leo's eyes widened as he looked at the man's face. "Geoff Hurst, as in the 1966 England legend?" mouthed Leo.

"That's the one," grinned Hurst. "I knew you'd get there in the end."

"Where are we?" asked Leo.

"We're in the back garden of the Hendon Hall Hotel," answered Hurst. "This used to be where the England team stayed before matches at Wembley Stadium."

"It's not very flash," frowned Leo.

Hurst laughed. "Things were
different in those days. It wasn't all
luxury hotels and huge expensive
homes. After we'd finished our playing
careers we couldn't just relax like

these younger lads nowadays. We had to get jobs. We needed to earn money to support our families."

"Sorry," said Leo, "but why am I here?"

"I've heard a rumour that you want to play centre forward for your school team."

"How do you know that?"

"Don't worry. I'm far more interested in whether or not you want to pick up some new skills as a striker. If not, then I'll be of no use to you."

"Y...y...yes," blurted out Leo. "I definitely do."

"Good answer," nodded Hurst. "The first thing I want to say is don't worry if you start a game as a sub. In my career, I spent plenty of matches on the bench."

Thoughts of Thursday's school match and Gavin Mathers boastful rant flickered through Leo's head.

"It happened to me at West Ham United, it happened to me with England. It doesn't mean anything. All that matters is that when you get some playing time you have to make the most of it, you have to make a difference. Do you understand?"

Leo nodded, trying to work out how he'd got to this place and why an England legend was bothering to take the time to talk to him.

"Well, if you're ready, I'm ready," said Hurst. "It's time for you to learn a thing or two about becoming a football hotshot."

CHAPTER 4
BECOMING A HOTSHOT

"OK," Hurst said, "the first thing we're going to focus on is controlling the ball before shooting."

Leo nodded eagerly.

"Your first touch is absolutely crucial. So many players in good shooting positions let themselves down with their first touch. But if you get it right, you're setting yourself up for the perfect shot. Get it on target and bam! You've scored."

Leo thought of Colombia's James Rodriguez, controlling the ball superbly with his chest and then firing in a sensational volley versus Uruguay at the 2014 World Cup finals in Brazil.

"Stand over there," said Hurst, pointing to a spot about ten metres away from him. "That wall over there is the goal. I'm going to throw you balls at different heights and angles. I want you to control the ball with one touch and then shoot with your second touch. It doesn't matter which part of your body you use to control it, but obviously not your hands."

"Got it," nodded Leo, smiling.

For the next half hour, Hurst chucked ball after ball at Leo. Some he couldn't control and they slipped away, but as time went by, Leo started controlling the ball with his head, his chest, his knees and his feet. Control to set up the shot; then smack it.

"That's a good start," said Hurst,

catching the ball. "We're ready to move onto the second key skill, and that's shooting on the run. It's all well and good scoring from stationary positions, but there'll be many times you'll need to shoot while running at speed."

"Cool," said Leo, still amazed that he was being coached by sensational centre forward Geoff Hurst.

For this exercise Hurst placed himself next to Leo, thirty metres away from the wall. "Right," said Hurst, "I'm a defender trying to get the ball off you. You have to outpace me and then strike the ball when you're moving at speed. Now go!"

And Leo did. He raced across the grass, ball at his feet, with Hurst racing

alongside him trying to snatch the ball. Over the course of the next hour, Hurst got in some good tackles, but Leo worked hard. He got used to evading Hurst's tackling and then taking shots when speeding down the field.

"Let's move onto the third part of this session," said Hurst, satisfied with how things were going so far. "We're going to focus on following through. To be a great striker, you don't just have to hit the ball well, you have to move your leg as if you're going to kick it right through the goal net; you need to follow through your shot with maximum power."

Leo nodded.

"I'm going to be in goal," said Hurst, "and I'll throw balls out to you. I want you to hit them on the ground, on the volley and on the half volley, but each time I want you to follow your shot through."

Leo's heart bounced around in excitement. He was about to take shots against Geoff Hurst!

Hurst stood in front of the wall and threw the ball to Leo. It bounced and he hit it on the half volley. His shot was OK, but it didn't have the power Hurst had talked about.

"Again!" commanded Hurst. Leo worked hard, and forty minutes later he was smashing in thunderous shots, his right leg following through for increased power.

"That's much better," called out Hurst, walking over to Leo. "We've now gone over the three most important skills for a striker: control before the shot, shooting on the run and follow through."

Leo didn't need reminding; he'd already seared them into his brain. Hurst whacked a ball high into the air in the direction of the hotel. "Let's see you catch up with that one," he grinned.

Leo raced across the grass to retrieve the ball, but when he got it and spun round, Hurst was nowhere to be seen. A split second later, the ground began trembling furiously. Leo closed his eyes as his body was flung onto the grass.

CHAPTER 5
TEAM SELECTION

When Leo opened his eyes he was sprawled out on the ground by the garages. There was no evidence of any earthquake. He stood up slowly and looked around for any signs of Geoff Hurst, but the star striker was gone.

Hurst's words rung in his mind:

"Control before the shot, shooting on the run, follow through."

If he stuck to those commands, maybe he'd have a chance of getting into the school team for Thursday's match.

* * * * * * * * * * * * * * * * * *

Leo was nervous during school the next day. A rumour was going round that Mr Cross would be announcing the team for Thursday's game, during after-school football practice.

In lunch break, when Leo and Mac were waiting in the canteen queue,

Gavin sidled over to them.

"I wouldn't bother putting yourself up for centre forward," said Gavin smugly. "Because that position will be going to me. Mr Cross has already told me."

"You're full of it," snapped Leo. He knew Mr Cross never gave any info out until everyone was together and he was ready.

"Yeah," nodded Mac, "and anyway, he'll choose players on ability, not on how loud they shoot their mouths off."

Gavin scowled and walked off.

"Nice one," grinned Leo.

* * * * * * * * * * * * * * * * *

Training was on the school field and when the players arrived Mr Cross wasn't around. In his place was Mr Lawson. He was a tall guy with large sideburns. Mac and Leo exchanged a shocked glance. Gavin stood a few metres away, looking ultra confident.

"OK, lads," said Mr Lawson. "I'm sorry I haven't spent much time with this team recently, but Mr Cross is looking after the seniors now, while I'm going to work with you."

"Yes!" whispered Leo under his breath.

Mr Lawson's coaching methods were very different from Mr Cross's. He didn't talk or shout out as much, but when he did it was to deliver very focused instructions. He also worked the players much harder. After half-an-hour of stretching, running and short passing, he organised two five-a-side games. Both Leo and Gavin said they'd like to try out as centre forward.

Leo and Mac were in one game. Gavin was in the other. Mr Lawson walked between the two games, watching everything like a bird of prey, and making notes on a clipboard.

Finally, he organised an eleven-a-side match. Leo was chosen as centre forward for one team, Gavin took the same position for the other team.

Leo had few touches in the first ten minutes, but then Mac raked the ball through the opposite team's defence and Leo sprinted towards it.

"Control before the shot, shooting on the run, follow through," Leo whispered to himself.

He reached the ball a second before a defender, touched it forward with his left leg and hit it with his right. It was a good strike, but the goalie dived to his left and caught the ball.

"Good effort!" shouted Mr Lawson.

Gavin glared at Leo.

Leo had a header cleared off the line just before half-time, and struck a decent volley near the end of the second half that hit the crossbar. Gavin had a scuffed shot saved and curled a free kick just wide of the left post.

When the final whistle went, Leo was confident that he'd played better than Gavin. Surely Mr Lawson would hand him the number 9 role on Thursday.

The players gathered around Mr Lawson in the centre circle. "Right," he said, looking from his clipboard to the expectant faces. "I obviously don't know you lot very well, but on the basis of today's session I've selected a team for Thursday's game against Heston College."

He had opted for a 4-5-1 formation. He read out the name of the keeper, and then the midfielders. Mac was awarded his favourite position in the centre right of midfield. Leo waited nervously.

"Please pick me ahead of Gavin," he said to himself.

"Playing at centre forward on Thursday," announced Mr Lawson, "will be...Gavin Mathers."

CHAPTER 6
ON THE SUBS BENCH

Leo felt as if the life had just been punched out of him. How could Mr Lawson pick Gavin, when Leo had clearly played miles better? It was so unfair!

As the team went to change Mac put an arm round Leo's shoulders. "Don't worry about it," said Mac. "Gavin will be rubbish and Mr Lawson will put you on."

Leo couldn't manage a smile or an answer to this. He just stared at Gavin, who was dancing around on the spot and telling anyone who would listen how he was going to be the next Neymar.

As Leo tramped back to the changing rooms, Mr Lawson walked up to him. "Don't look so downhearted, Leo," said the coach. "You did OK out there. I'd just like to see more powerful shooting from you. You had that good effort and I reckon if you'd followed through on your shot, you'd have scored."

Leo couldn't believe what he was hearing. Mr Lawson was criticising him over one of the skills Geoff Hurst had shown him. He should have followed that shot through. How could he have been so stupid!

* * * * * * * * * * * * * * * * * *

"What's up, Leo?" asked his mum, looking up from some paperwork she was studying. They were sitting on the small balcony, Leo with a look of thunder on his face.

"I didn't get picked for Thursday's match and I really thought I would. That idiot Gavin Mathers is playing instead."

"But you'll be on the subs bench, won't you?"

"Yeah, but I'll probably stay there for the whole game. It would be just my luck for Gavin to play a blinder and score the winning goal. Then I'll never get a game."

"I'm sure it won't happen like that," said his mum gently, "you're a great player. You're so dedicated to the game; you're always playing or training or working on your skills. Those things get rewarded. You deserve a break. Just...don't forget you're all on the same side."

Leo managed a half smile. "Thanks, Mum," he said, glad that she was supporting him, but not really believing a single word she said.

* * * * * * * * * * * * * * * * * *

The next day Leo moped about school. When Mac tried to talk to him he replied with one-word answers. When he got home he sat in his room looking at some stats for Geoff Hurst on his phone, but he couldn't really concentrate.

• Hurst made over 400 league appearances between 1959 and 1972, scoring 180 goals.

• Winner of the FA Cup (1964) and European Cup Winner's Cup (1965) with West Ham United.

• He played for American "soccer" side, the Seattle Sounders, in 1976, scoring 8 goals and making 4 assists in 23 games.

Leo kept imagining Gavin winning the game with a spectacular bicycle kick. He was in the middle of this bitter daydream when he glanced back at the photo of Hurst, his hair neatly combed and arms folded. Without warning,

Leo's bed began to shake. Books and school work spun into the air and he shielded his face to avoid being struck.

A second later the rumbling sound stopped and Leo opened his eyes.

He was standing on the touchline inside a football stadium on a sunny afternoon. He saw the stadium's two towers and recognised it as the old Wembley Stadium. On the terraces were people wearing clothes about fifty years out of date. Leo turned his gaze at the pitch and saw two teams battling it out — one in red shirts, the other in white.

And that's when it hit him.

This was no ordinary game.

It was the 1966 World Cup Final between England and West Germany!

CHAPTER 7
WEMBLEY, 1966

There with his hands on his hips was Geoff Hurst, decked out in his full England kit. He had an anxious look on his face. The ball had just gone out of play and a ball boy was racing to retrieve it.

Hurst saw Leo, smiled and then did something remarkable. He stepped from the outline of his body and ran straight over! Apart from Leo and Hurst it was obvious that no one else in the stadium had seen this.

"Delighted you could make it," said Hurst, patting Leo on the back. "Your timing is spot on."

"Why's that?" asked a shocked and

confused Leo.

"I'm scared that things are turning against us in this game," answered Hurst edgily.

"What's the score?" asked Leo.

"West Germany went 1—0 up on twelve minutes and then I scored with a header on eighteen minutes to level it at 1—1."

"And then?" asked Leo.

"In the seventy-seventh minute, a shot I hit was deflected and fell to Martin Peters, who smacked it in: 2—1. For the next twenty minutes we held our lead. Then on the eighty-ninth minute Wolfgang Weber knocked one in for the Germans: 2—2. The whistle for full time went very soon after, and shortly after that, we started extra time; we're five minutes in."

"What did your manager say?"

"Alf Ramsey is a man of few emotions, but he said one thing that hit us all like a rocket and raised our spirits. He said, 'You've won it once, now go and win it again.'"

"So why am I here?" asked Leo.

"My legs are losing the will to keep going," said Hurst. "I need a break and this is the perfect opportunity for you."

"ME?" blurted out Leo. "You want ME to play?"

"Absolutely!" nodded Hurst. "Take what I taught you; go out there and use those skills."

Leo couldn't believe what he was hearing. Geoff Hurst was instructing him to play in a World Cup Final — a

World Cup Final featuring England; it was madness. Hurst quickly went over the names of his team-mates so Leo would know who was who.

By now, the ball boy had got the ball and a throw-in was about to be taken.

"This is your moment!" urged Hurst. "Go and make some history!"

Leo took a deep breath, ran onto the pitch and stepped into Hurst's outline.

CHAPTER 8
GOAL-LINE DECISION

"Come on, lads!" shouted Jackie
Charlton from somewhere behind him.
"We can do this. We HAVE to do this!
There is NO WAY we are going to let our
country down!"

West Germany were passing the
brown leather ball around, looking for
a way to break through the England
defence. Leo was taken aback by the
running styles of the players and the
pace of the game in 1966; it seemed
slower than in the modern Premier
League.

Eleven minutes into extra time, a
small England player called Alan Ball,
with curly ginger hair, set off on a run

down the right flank. Leo raced forward
into the West German penalty area.
He had to be in the right place if Ball
managed a cross. Hurst's words buzzed
in his head. "Control before the shot,
shooting on the run, follow through."

Ball raced towards the by-line and floated in a cross. As Leo watched the ball fly through the air he knew what he was going to do. He brought the ball down with his right boot, and letting it roll a couple of paces forwards, Leo swivelled round. He smacked the ball hard with his right foot, following the shot through. As it left his boot he toppled over backwards.

Time seemed to stop for a second and then the ball hit the underside of the West German crossbar, bounced on the goal line and flew out.

"GOAL!" screamed Leo and his team-mates. The cap-wearing German goalkeeper, Hans Tilkowski walked out of his goal, looking bemused.

Leo got to his feet and raised his arm

in the air, but the referee didn't seem to know whether the ball had crossed the line fully. If this wasn't the case, the goal would be disallowed.

Leo was stunned. "Please don't rule it out," he thought in desperation.

The ref ran over to the linesman and had a quick discussion, using hand signals because they clearly didn't speak the same language. The ref then nodded his head, blew his whistle and pointed a finger towards the centre circle.

The goal stood!

The stadium erupted. The noise from the crowd was deafening.

Alan Ball ran straight over to Leo. Both of them were laughing and cheering.

England players surrounded Leo, chanting praise in his ears and grabbing him by the shoulders.

West German players pursued the ref, insisting that he and the linesman had got it wrong, but he waved them away.

Then Leo heard a voice that was

calmer and quieter than the rest. It was the England captain and defender supreme, Bobby Moore.

"It's nowhere near over!" he called out to his team-mates. "Don't forget they scored in the eighty-ninth minute and they'll go like crazy for another goal now. Let's keep our shape and win this game!"

Moore was a natural leader. He commanded total respect from his players. Leo nodded at Moore. Moore winked back.

A few seconds later everyone was ready for the restart; could England hold on or would West Germany nick the game?

CHAPTER 9
THEY THINK IT'S ALL OVER...

The first half of extra time was over a few minutes later, and England hadn't conceded. They were still winning 3–2. Leo grabbed a quick drink and Ramsey ordered the team to keep their discipline and shut the Germans out.

Before Leo knew it, the second half of extra time had started. It was clear that West Germany were going to attack, and they did in force. Leo tracked back to help the defence. Bobby Moore, Jack Charlton, George Cohen and Ray Wilson played superbly as a defensive four, with Nobby Stiles playing just ahead of them, going in for the crunching tackles and fending off

West Germany like a warrior.

Just then Leo heard someone on the England bench shouting out that there was just a minute left. One minute until England could win the ultimate football trophy.

A whistle sounded and loads of the players and spectators thought it was the ref's final whistle. But it had come from the crowd, and the ref waved play on.

At that second, a long ball was whacked out of the England penalty area. Leo was fifteen yards into the opposition's half. The ball hit the top of his shoulder and fell onto the pitch.

Control before the shot, shooting on the run, follow through.

Leo didn't need to be told what to do. He immediately started sprinting forwards with the ball at his feet, aware that a West German defender was racing after him. Dribbling at top speed he flew into the left side of the German penalty area, pushed the ball forward and struck it with as much power as he could muster with his left foot. He watched as the ball crashed into the top-left corner of the net. There was

no goal-line controversy this time, no agonised waiting for the ref's decision.

It was a goal — a brilliant goal.

The England players, the England staff and the England supporters went completely crazy. Their shrieks and cheers and clapping exploded around the stadium. The whole place was filled with waving arms and England flags. And in that moment, Leo realised he, along with the real Geoff Hurst, had scored a hat-trick and won the World Cup for England.

A few seconds later, the ref blew for full time and as some supporters raced onto the pitch, Leo felt a hand on his shoulder. He turned around and found Geoff Hurst standing beside him.

"You did it!" beamed Hurst. "You

took on everything I told you and you made the difference. No one in this stadium or throughout our country will ever forget what you just did."

"Thanks," smiled Leo, his heart pounding, his senses alive to the madness that had broken out around him.

"I reckon we'd better swap back now," laughed Hurst. "I can't miss getting my hands on that beautiful trophy."

They shook hands. Leo stepped out of the outline and Hurst walked back in.

A moment later, the Wembley turf began to shake violently. As grass flew into Leo's face he shut his eyes.

When he opened them, Wembley was gone. He was in his bedroom. The craziness of the 1966 World Cup Final had totally vanished.

CHAPTER 10
HOTSHOT SUB

The match against Heston College kicked off on Thursday after school. Gavin was playing centre forward while Mac was playing in midfield. Leo was a substitute, and he stood on the touchline, watching the action and feeling miserable.

The first thirty-five minutes were patchy. Both teams played nervously, neither wanting to concede a goal. To Leo's delight, Gavin had been marked out of the game by a tough Heston defender, which was great. But it did mean Leo's team hadn't managed many shots on goal.

Then Mac wrested the ball from one

of the Heston strikers and floated a pass upfield. Gavin chested the ball down and raced round the Heston right back.

Mac sprung forwards to join the attack.

Gavin cut inside another defender and entered the penalty area.

"Over here!" yelled Mac, waving his right arm.

Gavin had a quick look up, feigned a pass to Mac and then struck the ball. It wasn't a great strike, but it rolled under the keeper's body and trickled into the net.

Gavin raised his arms in the air and shouted with joy. As he ran back for the Heston kickoff, he grinned at Leo on the touchline and hissed, "You could never have done that!"

Leo seethed with fury, while Mr Lawson looked on.

Soon it was half-time with the scoreline at 1–0. Gavin strutted around as if he was the most important player in the team.

Mr Lawson did the half-time team

talk, concentrating on the defence because it had lost its shape and discipline on a few occasions. Then he turned to the attack.

Gavin grinned, waiting for the praise.

But Mr Lawson's face suddenly looked deadly serious.

"Our attack has been far too static," began Mr Lawson. "We need more movement to slip away from that Heston defender. Plus, we need someone willing to track back and support the defence. Gavin, you're off. Leo, you're playing upfront in the second half."

A stunned Gavin said in a trembling voice. "B...b...but I scored the only goal."

"You did," nodded Mr Lawson, "but we need to talk about your team spirit

— there's no room for individuals, we play as a team."

Gavin looked as if he'd just been sat on by a hippo.

Leo's spirits soared dramatically, and a few minutes later he was lining up for the kickoff.

Control before the shot, shooting on the run, follow through.

He had to heed these words.

For ten minutes Leo hardly had the ball, despite his movement. Then it was fed to him in the centre circle. He trapped the ball with his left instep and then started running at the Heston defence. He rounded one player and then another backed away from him. He was now bearing down on the penalty area. He made as if to shoot, but then slid the ball to Mac, who thumped it into the top-right corner.

"Amazing pass!" grinned Mac, high-fiving with Leo.

"Amazing goal!" laughed Leo.

Gavin sat on the substitutes bench looking like a poodle in a rainstorm.

For twenty minutes it was end-to-end stuff and after a defensive error, Heston pulled a goal back: 2—1.

It was a midfield battle after this, but with five minutes remaining, Leo's keeper took a mighty goal kick. Leo was just inside the Heston half and he started hurtling towards the Heston goal.

The ball bounced just in front of him. He flicked it over a defender and brought it down with his chest. As Leo raced into the penalty area, two

Heston defenders sprinted to close him down. He knew what he had to do. He pushed the ball slightly ahead, pulled back his left foot and blasted the ball with a follow-through for power. The ball sailed between the defenders

and beat the goalie into the top-left corner: 3−1!

Leo's team-mates went mad, leaping on him and screaming wildly.

"Top goal, Leo," called out Mr Lawson. "Great technique!"

Leo ran back to his own half, noticing a furious-looking Gavin, who was standing on the touchline. "So what, Leo?" Gavin shouted. "It's not the World Cup Final!"

Leo ignored him and got ready for the kickoff. He'd learnt with the hottest shot of them all — the only player to score a hat-trick in a World Cup Final. Nothing could take that away. And besides, there were still five minutes left of this game to play. Plenty of time to score another goal.

FOOTBALL STAR POWER

There are four books to collect!

Free-kick Pro

Jonny Zucker

978 1 4451 2615 9 pb   978 1 4451 2619 7 ebook

Demon Dribbler

Jonny Zucker

978 1 4451 2616 6 pb   978 1 4451 2620 3 ebook

Driving Force

Jonny Zucker

978 1 4451 2617 3 pb   978 1 4451 2621 0 ebook

Hottest Shot

Jonny Zucker

978 1 4451 2618 0 pb   978 1 4451 2622 7 ebook